For Harry & Elsie — natural bubblers! —M.M.

For Holly, Craig & Marbles — P.D.

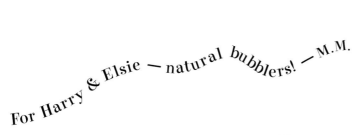

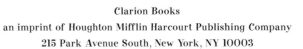

Clarion Books
an imprint of Houghton Mifflin Harcourt Publishing Company
215 Park Avenue South, New York, NY 10003

Text copyright © 2008 by Margaret Mahy
Illustrations copyright © 2008 by Polly Dunbar
First published in the United Kingdom in 2008 by Frances Lincoln Limited.
First American edition, 2009.

SCRABBLE® is a registered trademark. All intellectual property rights in and to the game are owned
in the U.S.A. and Canada by Hasbro Inc. and throughout the rest of the world by J.W. Spear & Sons, PLC of Enfield,
Middlesex, England, a subsidiary of Mattel Inc. Mattel and Spear are not affiliated with Hasbro.

The illustrations were executed in watercolors and cut paper.
The text was set in 18-point Elroy.

www.clarionbooks.com

Printed in Singapore.

Library of Congress Cataloging-in-Publication Data
Mahy, Margaret.
Bubble trouble / Margaret Mahy ; illustrated by Polly Dunbar. —1st American ed.
p. cm
Summary: Mabel blows a bubble that captures Baby and wafts him away,
resulting in a wild chase that involves the whole neighborhood.
ISBN 978-0-547-07421-4
[1. Stories in rhyme. 2. Bubbles—Fiction. 3. Humorous stories.] I. Dunbar, Polly, ill. II. Title.
PZ8.3.M278 Bu 2009
[E]—22        2008007244

10  9  8  7  6  5  4  3  2  1

# BUBBLE TROUBLE

by

Margaret Mahy

Illustrated by

Polly Dunbar

Clarion Books • New York

LITTLE MABEL blew a bubble, and it caused a lot of trouble...

Such a lot of bubble trouble in a bibble-bobble way.

For it broke away from Mabel as it bobbed across the table,

where it bobbled over Baby, and it wafted him away.

6

The baby didn't quibble. He began to smile and dribble,
for he liked the wibble-wobble of the bubble in the air.
But Mabel ran for cover as the bubble bobbed above her,
and she shouted out for Mother, who was putting up her hair.

At the sudden cry of trouble, Mother took off at the double, for the squealing left her reeling, made her terrified and tense, saw the bubble for a minute, with the baby bobbing in it, as it bibbled by the letterbox and bobbed across the fence.

In her garden, Chrysta Gribble had begun to cry and cavil at her lazy brother, Greville, reading novels in his bed.

But she bellowed,
"Gracious, Greville!"
and she groveled on the gravel

when the baby in the bubble
bibble-bobbled overhead.

11

In a garden folly, Tybal and his jolly mother, Sybil,
sat and played a game of Scrabble, shouting shrilly as they scored.
But they both began to babble and to scrobble with the Scrabble
as the baby in the bubble bibble-bobbled by the board.

12

Then crumpled Mr. Copple and his wife (a crabby couple)
set out arm in arm to hobble and to squabble down the lane.
But the baby in the bubble turned their hobble to a joggle
as they raced away like rockets—and they've never limped again.

Even feeble Mrs. Threeble, in a muddle with her needle (matching pink and purple patches for a pretty patchwork quilt), when her older sister told her, tossed the quilt across her shoulder, as she set off at a totter in her tattered tartan kilt.

16

At the shops, a busy rabble met to gossip and to gabble,

started gibbering and goggling as the bubble bobbled by.

Mother, hand in hand with Mabel, flew as fast as she was able,

very troubled lest the bubble burst or vanish in the sky.

After them came Greville Gribble in his nightshirt with his novel

(all about a haunted hovel) held on high above his head,

followed by his sister, Chrysta (though her boots had made a blister),

then came Tybal, pulling Sybil, with the Scrabble for a sled.

After them the Copple couple came cavorting at the double,

then a jogger (quite a slogger) joined the crowd, who called and coughed.

Up above the puzzled people—way up toward the chapel steeple—

rose the bubble (with the baby) slowly lifting up aloft.

There was such a flum-a-diddle (Mabel huddled in the middle),
Canon Dapple left the chapel, followed by the chapel choir.
And the treble singer Abel threw an apple core at Mabel,

as the baby in the bubble bobbled up a little higher.

Oh, they giggled and they goggled until all their brains were boggled,

as the baby in the bubble rose above the little town.

"With the problem let us grapple," murmured kindly Canon Dapple,

"and the problem we must grapple with is bringing Baby down."

"Now, let Mabel stand on Abel, who could stand in turn on Tybal,

who could stand on Greville Gribble, who could stand upon the wall,

while the people from the shop'll stand to catch them if they topple,

then perhaps they'll reach the bubble, saving Baby from a fall."

But Abel, though a treble, was a rascal and a rebel,

fond of getting into trouble when he didn't have to sing.

Pushing quickly through the people, Abel clambered up the steeple

with nefarious intentions and a pebble in his sling!

Abel quietly aimed the pebble past the steeple of the chapel,
at the baby in the bubble wibble-wobbling way up there.
And the pebble burst the bubble! So the future seemed to fizzle
for the baby boy, who grizzled as he tumbled through the air.

What a moment for a mother as her infant plunged above her!

There were groans and gasps and gargles from the horror-stricken crowd.

Sybil said, "Upon my honor, there's a baby who's a goner!"
And Chrysta hissed with emphasis, "It shouldn't be allowed!"

But Mabel, Tybal, Greville, and the jogger (christened Neville)
didn't quiver, didn't quaver, didn't drivel, shrivel, wilt.
But as one they made a swivel, and with action (firm but civil)
they divested Mrs. Threeble of her pretty patchwork quilt.

Oh, what calculated catchwork! Baby bounced into the patchwork,
where his grizzles turned to giggles and to wriggles of delight!
And the people stared dumbfounded as he bobbled and rebounded,
till the baby boy was grounded and his mother held him tight.

34

And the people there still prattle—there is lots of tittle-tattle—

for the glory in the story, young and old folk, gold and gray,

of how wicked treble Abel tripled trouble with his pebble,

but how Mabel (and some others) saved her brother and the day.